Lolly LaCrumb's Cupcake Adventure

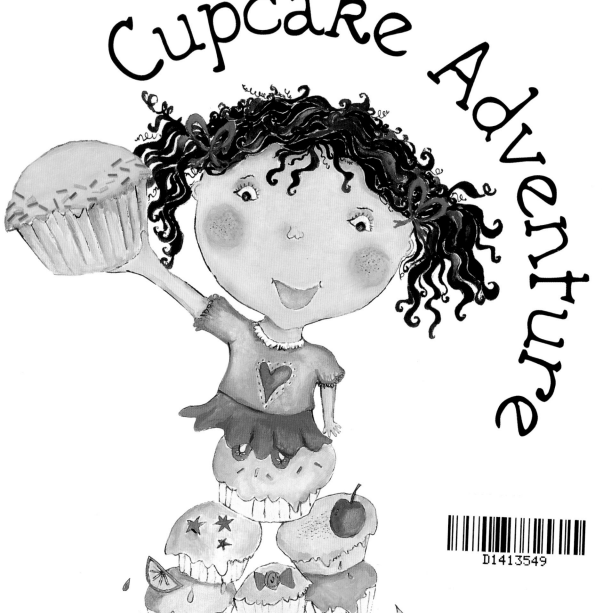

Lolly's mom kissed her head and said with delight, "Happy Birthday Lolly!"

Lolly was so excited, she jumped out of bed.
She wondered if her birthday breakfast
would just be oatmeal or if it might be
something special.

Lolly's mom offered her cereal, bananas, eggs, a muffin, and even some toast. Then Lolly suddenly remembered her dream. In it she had seen the most perfect cupcake, piled high with pink frosting. But Lolly's mom explained, "Cupcakes aren't really for breakfast, even a special birthday breakfast."

So, Lolly hopped on her bike and headed for the store. She was certain she would find what she wanted. Her tummy rumbled a little and she could almost taste the frosting.

Outside the store, Lolly saw Sandy, Billy, and Sue eating cookies and snacks. She explained to them, "Today is my birthday and I want to find the perfect cupcake."

But hard as Lolly searched, she couldn't find
any cupcakes. "Oh dear! No cupcake here,"
Lolly said, and off she sped.

Lolly passed Uncle Blake's house and found him hard at work. "Happy Birthday Lolly! Can I get you some cake?" said Uncle Blake. With this Lolly let out a sigh and shook her head.

Even Auntie Vi was no help. All she had to offer was pie. "Oh dear! No cupcake here," Lolly said, and off she sped.

Lolly had to think where to go next and
remembered Miss Lilly O'Barre, the famous star!
She had such a big house and so many cooks.

Lolly ran inside, but there was not a cupcake in sight, only fancy desserts with custards, and creams, and raspberry puddings. "Oh dear! No cupcake here," Lolly said, and off she sped.

Then a firetruck raced by and Lolly had an idea. She should head to the firehouse to see Buck and his dad.

When she got there, Lyle, the black and white Dalmatian, jumped up to say hello.

Fireman Tuck and his son, Buck greeted her with
big smiles. But Lolly could see that there were no
cupcakes here and a little tear ran down her cheek.
"Oh dear! No cupcake here," Lolly said, and off she sped.

Lolly thought she was never going to find her perfect birthday cupcake. And as she reached over to scratch an itch, her bike skidded and fell in a ditch!

"Figures!" cried Lolly as she lay on
her back to catch her breath.

Lolly left her bike and walked the rest of the way home. Her head was hanging low when she reached Bradley Cook's house, next door to her own. But then she had another idea. Maybe Bradley's mom would have her perfect cupcake!

Bradley's mom baked lots of brownies.
But that was all. So with a sigh, Lolly said,
"Oh dear! No cupcake here!" and with that she
decided to give up her search and go home.

And when she arrived, she couldn't believe her eyes! There was her perfect birthday cupcake exactly like the one in her dream. As she looked around at all of her friends she cried with delight, "This is the best birthday ever!"

And at that moment, Lolly realized that the one thing that would make her even happier and bring her all that she really wanted...

would be to share her cupcake

with all of her friends!